Winner Books are produced by Victor Books and are designed to entertain and instruct young readers in Christian principles. Each book has been approved by specialists in Christian education and children's literature. These books uphold the teachings and principles of the Bible.

Other Winner Books you will enjoy:

Sarah and the Magic Twenty-fifth, by Margaret Epp
Sarah and the Lost Friendship, by Margaret Epp
Sarah and the Mystery of the Hidden Boy, by Margaret Epp
Sarah and the Darnley Boys, by Margaret Epp
Sarah and the Pelican, by Margaret Epp
The Hairy Brown Angel and Other Animal Tails, edited by Grace Fox Anderson
The Peanut Butter Hamster and Other Animal Tails, edited by Grace Fox Anderson
Danger on the Alaskan Trail (three mysteries)
Gopher Hole Treasure Hunt, by Ralph Bartholomew
Daddy, Come Home, by Irene Aiken
Battle at the Blue Line, by P.C. Fredricks
Patches, by Edith Buck
The Taming of Cheetah, by Lee Roddy
Ted and the Secret Club, by Bernard Palmer
The Giant Trunk Mystery, by Linda Boorman
Colby Moves West, by Sharon Miller

Mother of three, a children's worker in her church, and a former public school teacher, LINDA BOORMAN has shared stories with children for 20 years. Now she is writing her own, and her unusual sense of humor makes her stories delightful.

Mrs. Boorman lives in Frenchtown, Montana. She is a graduate of Multnoma School of the Bible and received her B.S. in Education from Eastern Oregon State College. Her earlier years were spent near small Oregon towns similar to the fictitious Horseshoe Bend of this first novel.

The Mystery Man of Horseshoe Bend

by Linda Boorman

illustrated by
Marilee Harrald

A WINNER BOOK

VICTOR BOOKS
a division of SP Publications, Inc.
WHEATON. ILLINOIS 60187

Offices also in Fullerton, California • Whitby, Ontario, Canada • Amersham-on-the-Hill, Bucks, England

Second printing, 1981

All Scripture quotations are from the King James Version.

Library of Congress Catalog Card Number: 79-55320
ISBN: 0-88207-488-1

VICTOR BOOKS
A division of SP Publications, Inc.
P.O. Box 1825, Wheaton, Ill. 60187

Contents

1
Bicycle
Thief

IT WAS a warm June evening in 1897. School had let out just the week before, so I had no homework to do. I was perched, unladylike,* on our front porch railing, wishing something exciting would happen. Nothing *ever* seemed to happen in our lazy little Oregon town of Horseshoe Bend.* Well, not very often, anyway.

It's true that living in the parsonage * did bring

Whenever you see a star, you'll know you can find more information or an explanation about the word or place under Life in 1897 on pages 93-100.

us some interesting visitors now and then. But right now I was bored. Take Sidney Wright, for instance. He was sweet on my oldest sister Sarah. They worked together at his father's drugstore.* Each evening he came courting * as regularly as the sun set.

I could see just his head as he walked along his usual route on the other side of our lilac bushes. But what a surprise I had when he reached the gate! He was pushing a shiny, new black *bicycle!**

I leaped off the railing and dashed out to meet him. "Sidney! Where'd you get it?" I screeched.

He smiled in his usual uppity way. "Sent back East for it," he said. "Spent all day Saturday putting it together. It's a beauty, isn't it!" He whisked out his hanky * and dusted off the nickle-plated handlebars.

"It sure is," I agreed. "But why aren't you riding it?"

He carefully leaned the bicycle against the porch, then dabbed at each of his fingers with his hanky. "I'm in the process of learning," he said. "It's really quite complicated."

"I'm sure I could ride without any trouble," I declared with the confidence of the inexperienced. "I've been studying up on bicycles in *Collier's Encyclopedia of Social Information and Treasury of*

Useful and Entertaining Knowledge. I've read all three lessons on riding bicycles. Even the part on how to ride without hands—"

Sidney barely listened to my chatter. Instead, he gave each side of his mustache a little twirl, then skipped up the steps.

I moved over to his bicycle, eyeing it eagerly. What I'd told him was true. Ever since I'd first seen one pictured in the *Sears and Roebuck Catalog,* I'd been reading everything I could get my hands on about bicycles.

My twin brother Tommy's encyclopedia and his "Scientific American" magazine said quite a lot about bicycles. And the new *Sears and Roebuck Catalog* showed several splendid models.

Of course, with my father the preacher at Horseshoe Bend Community Church, I couldn't afford even a bicycle bell or light, let alone a bicycle. But I'd been praying for a miracle. And now, here was a bicycle—the first I'd ever seen up close.

I ran my hands over the smooth, cold bars. I was just considering flipping my leg over the long bar when . Tommy dashed around the house. Tommy, like the rest of us Conroys—except Mama and Sarah—has red hair and freckles.

He came to a screeching stop. "Susie, where'd the bicycle come from?" he cried.

"It's Sidney's. He sent back East for it. Hold it for me, Tommy. I want to get on the seat."

Tommy was always sensible and more careful than I was. "Susie, you'd better not," he said. "Sidney's pretty fussy about his things. Move over and let me look at it."

Reluctantly, I moved back, and he knelt down and examined the pedals and chain.

"Tommy, I'd give my perfect attendance award to ride a bicycle," I told him.

But he was too interested in checking over the bicycle to hear me.

"Hmmm, so that's how it runs," he mumbled, straightening up. "Someday I'll build one."

And I didn't doubt it, knowing his "mechanical" mind.

"We've got to spade the garden now until it gets dark," he told me. "C'mon. Aunt Minnie sent me after you."

I followed Tommy slowly out to the garden in back of the large "frazzled around the edges" parsonage. Nine of us Irish * Conroys lived there. (That included Aunt Minnie, Papa's sister. She had come to live with us when Tommy and I were born. Her hunch that twins would be a life-long job had proved true.)

While breaking up clods with Papa's shovel, I

went over and over in my mind the points given in the encyclopedia on bicycle riding. Later that evening I reread the chapter on "Lessons in Bicycle Riding." It seemed to me that a person would only need to take a bicycle to the top of a hill and coast down. The rest would come easy.

That night I dreamed I pedaled right up to Sidney on his bicycle. He clapped and smiled with approval. But I've noticed that dreams are usually pretty silly.

The next morning, I had to work in the garden again. After I'd finished, Mama asked me to go down the street to the Grand Hotel. Abby, my next-to-the-oldest sister, works at the hotel. I was to give her a message. But she never got it.

As I skipped out our back door and around the house, I nearly tripped over Sidney's bicycle. It was leaning against the porch, just like last night.

I heard Sidney's voice coming from the far end of the porch: "Things were slow at the store this morning, Sarah, so Father sent me over to tell you he won't need you today. Which brings me back to our discussion last evening. I *do* need you by my side—"

Wow, that sounded interesting enough to stay and listen to. But I just had to try out Sidney's bicycle. I lifted the skirt of my dress and swung my leg over the bicycle bar. And immediately lost my balance.

If I hadn't grabbed the porch railing when I did, the bicycle would have tipped over. Its skinny tires made staying up a bit of a problem, I found. But from my reading, I was sure that, once in motion, the bicycle would be easy to balance.

The voices on the porch had become whispers. I got off the bike, turned it around, and pushed it quietly out the back way. The steep road up to Horseshoe Bend's cemetery ran right past our house and the church next door. I figured I'd push the bike up there, then ride it down the hill. I'd have it leaning against the porch before Sidney and Sarah finished gazing into each other's eyes.

The bicycle grew heavier with each step up "Cemetery Hill." By the time I reached the gate at the top, my dress clung to me in wet patches, and I was gasping for breath.

When I turned around and looked down the hill, I had some second thoughts. It wasn't the best-kept, smoothest road * in the country. It was used mostly for funerals and on Decoration Day.* But I had to get Sidney's bicycle back to the parsonage. And the easiest way seemed to be by getting on and coasting downhill.

I stepped up on a rock, then swung onto the seat. With a little push, I was off!

The whirlwind swishing Elijah and his fiery chariot to heaven couldn't have been much more exciting. I never had a chance to touch the pedals. My legs stuck straight out, while the rushing air blew back my long red braids and ballooned out the skirt of my dress.

Every time the bicycle hit a rock or a hole in the road, I soared off the seat and expected to end up eye-level with the birds. But I always came down with a thump that jarred my teeth.

No wonder they called bicycles "boneshakers"!* This one seemed to shake all the facts on "how to ride a bicycle" and "how to stop a bicycle" right out of my head.

Before I knew it we—the bicycle and I—were nearing the bottom of the hill where the road curved sharply to the right. The road curved, that is, but the bicycle and I didn't.

There's a large elderberry bush right there at that curve. Landing in it would have helped break my fall. Instead, I landed on the rock in the middle of the bush and nearly ruined both the bike and me.

Though bleeding and bruised, I did manage to pick myself up. But I was sick when I saw that I'd broken some of the spokes of the front wheel and bent the wheel out of shape.

Unfortunately, Sidney and Sarah's heart to heart talk must not have lasted very long. Sidney was the one I met out in front of the house as I hobbled up, pushing the banged up bicycle.

Once Sidney recovered from the shock of seeing his new bicycle battered, he knelt down and went over it, exclaiming, "My new bicycle! Look at it! What will I do with it? Where will I get parts? It will never be the same again. Look at that wheel." Suddenly he remembered that I was there—and responsible for the damage.

He stood up and glared at me. "Susanne Conroy, how *could* you take my bicycle without my permission? And whatever made you think you could ride it?" he demanded.

"I th-thought coasting down Cemetery Hill would be easy—b-but it didn't work out like I figured," I stammered, feeling just awful.

Sidney took the bicycle from me and half-carried, half-pushed it off down the street. Meanwhile, I slunk around to the back door of the parsonage, hoping no one would see me.

But naturally I ran smack into Aunt Minnie. "Bless me, and what have we here!" she cried. "And if your dress isn't torn and your chin bleeding!"

Her sympathetic tone almost brought me to tears. But when I didn't answer, she became suspicious. "Susanne Conroy, what shenanigans * have you been up to now?" She emphasized the "now." She couldn't understand why at 12 I couldn't be a lady like Sarah or Abby.

I ducked under her arm and into the house and was almost across the kitchen when Papa came striding through the hall toward me. I stopped dead in my tracks.

"Well now, Susie, what have you to say for yourself!" he began, as he planted himself directly in front of me. "My daughter—a common thief. 'Tis past believing that a Conroy would bring such shame on the name of our Lord and our family—and on the parsonage."

"How did you kn-now, Papa?" I asked.

"I met Sidney on the street and he told me the whole story," he said.

"Tattletale," I muttered under my breath.

Just then Mama stepped into the room, and Sarah, hearing Sidney's name mentioned, came flying in. Five-year-old Joey followed her and walked around me saying such things as, "Susie, your chin's bleeding, and your dress is ripped. Look at that dirt all over her."

But the others—Aunt Minnie, Papa, and Sarah

—all talked at once. All accusing and exclaiming. Only Mama stood there silent. Her blue eyes were wide and sad and she'd shake her head occasionally as Papa told what I'd done. Her silence and disappointment were harder to take than all the others' hollering.

In the end, I was almost glad to follow Papa out to the woodshed for my punishment. I *was* anyway until he started firing Bible verses at me. Verses like "Thou shalt not covet" and "Thou shalt not steal" and "Honor thy father and thy mother" were hard to take just then.

Then he reminded me of Jesus' love and forgiveness for sinners like me, and I was crying long before he gave me the switching. When he got done, I supposed my troubles were the worst in recorded history. How was I to know they'd only begun?

2
The Shifty-eyed Bicycle Salesman

THAT AFTERNOON I was pretty unhappy. It seemed as if the whole world was against me. When Papa was through, I had to go to my room without lunch. I had just come out to sit on the porch because my room upstairs was so warm.

I was slouched in the porch rocker when this tall, skinny young man walked up the steps and leaned over me. "Is this where the parson* lives?" he asked.

Contrary to all Mama's lessons in deportment,* I remained in the same unladylike position. "Yup, but he's gone out to the Miller ranch to help Grandma Miller die."

He straightened up, frowning, and I dragged myself to my feet. My eyes were about level with his belt buckle, though I was the tallest in our sixth-reader class when school let out only two weeks back.

Wow, a real human beanpole! I thought. But aloud I said, "She dies about once a week and always wants the preacher."

He relaxed a moment, then his Adam's apple took an alarming jump as he cleared his throat and rattled off, "As it happens, I'm selling the world's most outstanding bicycles and—"

"Bicycles!" I shrieked. "That's why I'm in trouble —all because of a bicycle."

The front screen door banged against the side of the house, and Aunt Minnie stomped out, looking mad enough to sour cream. "Susie Conroy! Sure and 'twould seem you had enough misfortune today. And now a big 12-year-old a-yelling like a wild Indian."

She stopped, looked that bag of bones up and down, and forgot all about me. "Sure and you're lookin' like a beggar, young man," she said. "I've some stew to the back of the stove." And with that she shoved him through the door to the kitchen, and I followed. (Aunt Minnie would feed the enemy army if they looked hungry.)

He told us his name was Abraham Lincoln Brown. He was traveling across the West, selling bicycles from his van.* Since bicycles were all the rage in the East he was sure that the inhabitants of eastern Oregon would want to get in on the healthful fun they provided.

It was obvious he didn't know much about Horse-shoe Bend. Maybe bicycles were selling big back East, but I doubted he'd sell many around here. Oh, sure, I had my heart set on one. But after the morning's calamity, my getting one was about as likely as Sidney's forgiveness.

I sat down at the table and propped my head up on the palms of my hands and studied Mr. Brown. When your father is a preacher and your house is the first one after crossing the bridge into town, entertaining travelers is as common as flies. But though he gobbled up Aunt Minnie's stew the same as any hungry guest, I knew from the first he was different.

All the homey smells and sounds of Aunt Minnie's kitchen seemed to laugh at the notion. But the fire crackling under the Irish stew and the aroma of newly baked bread couldn't keep me from the feeling that Mr. Brown might not be quite trustworthy. Maybe it was the way he peered out from under his straggly blond hair and kept looking around the room like a caged animal.

I jumped when Mama laid her hand on my shoulder. She always moves quietly among us noisy Conroys. She'd just come from napping, because she suffers from a weak constitution.

Aunt Minnie stopped waving her hands around and pouring out advice when she saw Mama. "Mr. Brown, this be the lady of the house, Mrs. Conroy."

I've noticed that most mothers aren't pretty like mine. Even Mr. Brown seemed to appreciate her silky black hair and creamy complexion. His squinty eyes opened wider when Mama told him how pleased she was to meet him.

I think she's the kind of woman God talks about in the Bible in Proverbs, and I long to be like her. But the minute I'm out of her sight, I act just like a Conroy—loud and clumsy.

Mama politely excused us. Then, leaving Aunt Minnie to entertain our bicycle salesman, she drew me into her bedroom.

She raised the dark green shades in order to better examine my wounds. She'd cleaned them up after Papa was through with me, but with all the commotion, she hadn't had an opportunity to talk to me.

She seated me on a chair and raised the hem of my dress. Tenderly, Mama touched my swollen knees. I'd ruined the knees of my winter under-drawers,* but I doubted that she'd scold me for that. They were too small and spring seemed to be here at last.

"My back part hurts the worst," I told her, referring to the part Papa had used the willow switch on. (He'd told me he was sorry he had to use it on someone my age, but stealing called for harsh measures.)

Mama looked up and shook her head slightly. "Susie, whatever made you take Sidney Wright's bicycle?"

"Mama, I've wanted to ride a bicycle for *years*. So, when I saw it leaning against the porch, I just took it. Sidney was so busy mooning * over Sarah, he never saw me."

"But to take it all the way to the top of Cemetery Hill! Then to lose control while coming down. And ruining those spokes!"

"As punishment, I've got to clean Wright's Drugstore all summer to pay for the spokes," I told her. That was one of the things Papa had worked out with Sidney after our "talk." Being around that dandified * Sidney every day would be punishment in itself.

I squeaked as Mama pushed up my sleeve and surveyed my damaged elbow.

"Even so, Mama, I *do* wish I had a bicycle to ride. Until the crash, that ride was breathtaking, even better than jumping out of a hayloft."

Mama raised one black eyebrow. "They say ladies back East ride all around. I suppose times are changing, but straddling a bicycle hardly seems proper." She looked me right in the eye, and I wondered if she was sorry her youngest daughter had turned into a clumsy thief.

But she put her arm around me and gave me a little squeeze. "Never mind. Your getting a bicycle is highly unlikely, even if we *are* entertaining a bicycle salesman."

I sighed, knowing she was right.

"Susie, you must learn to think before you act. Look before you leap. Isn't that how the saying goes?"

"Or before you straddle and skedaddle,"* I said, my good humor returning.

Mama didn't bother to answer as she picked up her Bible. "Now I have a bit of Scripture I want you to apply to yourself. Let's see, it's right here in Psalm 25:3. The first part says, 'Yea, let none that wait on Thee [meaning God] be ashamed.'"

"That's easy," I said, wondering why she gave

someone who'd learned whole chapters such a little verse. "I can say it right now."

"I don't want you to *recite* it to me, Susie," Mama said. "I want you to make it so much a part of you that you live it."

I promised her I'd try, but I knew it wouldn't be easy.

Our scrawny visitor with the shifty eyes had been invited to put up his horse in the stable and park his van (which he lived in) beside it.

The first chance I had, I went to look at his bicycles. Close up, the van looked as sorry as its owner. A large sign, now faded and peeling, had been painted on each side. The peeling paint advertised, "World's Best Flyer Bicycle." Flying—just how I'd described the wonderful feeling I'd had when coming down Cemetery Hill.

It occurred to me that I might offer myself as a saleslady. If I worked hard, maybe I could earn a Flyer bicycle.

The door at the back of the van was open, so I stood on tiptoes to see inside. But before my eyes had a chance to adjust to the gloomy inside, long bony fingers dug into my shoulder.

3
Mrs. C
and the
Gold
Coins

I LOOKED UP into Mr. Brown's scowling face. "What're you doin' snooping around here?"

"I—I wanted to see your bicycles. After all, I'm probably more interested in bicycles than anyone else in Horseshoe Bend. I could help you sell them. I've ridden before (no sense going into the details, I figured) and I'd be willing to be your assistant. If you haven't any money," I continued breathlessly, "I'd be glad to take it out in merchandise."

"NO! Get out of here," he said. "I'll take care of my business and you mind yours."

I got out of there before my Irish temper had

24

time to rise. I'd done enough to be ashamed of for one day.

I needed Tommy. Even though we were born on the same day and look alike, our similarities end there. He's a thinker and inventor and not as hare-brained* as I am.

I found him busy, inventing an automatic door opener for Aunt Minnie. (She has the habit of trying to get out the back door with both hands full of pig scraps, clothes for the line, or kindling.*) Tommy squatted under the French lilac bush by the back door, banging away at a pile of wires and springs.

"Tommy," I said. But he didn't look up. I tried again. "Tommy!" Still no answer. "TOMMY!" I yelled. Tommy and his one-track mind! He didn't even know I was there. I broke a sprig of lilac blossoms off and sniffed its spicy scent.

When Tommy stopped banging, I rapped him on the head with the flowers. "Tommy, would you listen?" I said. "I smell a rat. That bicycle salesman won't show me even one of his bicycles."

Tommy took Papa's pliers and yanked a wire around. "He probably knows you're as poor as Job's turkey."

"But I offered to *sell* bicycles. And he needn't have been so rude."

"Susie, would you mind getting off that spring," Tommy said.

I could see that he wouldn't be any help until he'd finished tinkering with that pile of junk.

By suppertime, everyone but Sarah was in fine humor again. Nine of us, plus one bicycle salesman, sat down to enjoy Aunt Minnie's chicken and dumplings that night.

Sarah's black looks told me that she found my "borrowing" her prospective husband's bicycle inexcusable. (Sarah's trouble is that she inherited Mama's good looks, but not her good nature.)

"Papa, I heard the most exciting news at the hotel!" Abby exclaimed, as soon as Papa finished asking the blessing.

"And what might that be? President Cleveland plans to sleep in the hotel's grand suite?" Papa asked.

"Of course not," Abby said, laughing. "I heard that we have enough money in the bell fund at church to buy a bell. And," she shook her finger at Papa, "to think the preacher's daughter had to learn about it from hotel gossip."

Her news took my mind off my future encounter with Sarah.

"Sure and I was meaning to surprise everyone at prayer meeting tomorrow night." Papa turned to

Mr. Brown and said, "There's no keeping secrets in Horseshoe Bend, my friend."

Abe Brown, who was poking a piece of chicken breast into his mouth, choked. Aunt Minnie leaped up and slapped him on the back, almost knocking him out of his chair.

Mama and Sarah winced at her coarse behavior.

" 'Tis past believing, but there was a $50 gold piece in last Sunday's offering," Papa continued, ignoring the commotion.

That astonishing news silenced all 10 of us.

I could hear the wings of a moth fluttering around the oil lamp and old Sniffer—our dog—snoring near my feet. I nudged him with my toe to warn him that he'd better stop. If he didn't, Aunt Minnie would threaten to cut off his tail behind his ears as she scooted him out the back screen door.

Even Timmy stopped kicking his highchair.

Suddenly, Joe, who's five and often forgets that children are to be seen and not heard, sang out, "I know who gave it. I saw Mrs. Clackenbush drop it in."

"And are you sure of that, Joseph?" Aunt Minnie asked. "She can hardly keep soul and body together; God bless her. Now where and all would she be coming up with a $50 gold piece?"

"Aunt Minnie, I got good eyes. You told me I could see like a hawk," Joe declared.

I was as amazed as Aunt Minnie. Tiny, church-mouse-poor Mrs. Clackenbush (whom we call Mrs. C, for short) owning a $50 gold piece? Why, I could picture myself with a new bicycle before I could imagine that. The only thing Mrs. C has a lot of is cats. Her tumbledown log cabin is always overrun with every kind of cat known to man and a few that aren't.

"She sure don't tell none of her affairs," Aunt Minnie said, sniffing. (People less talkative than herself always upset Aunt Minnie.)

Papa ran his fingers through his bushy red hair, a sure sign that he was as puzzled as the rest of us.

"Are you talking about Effie Mae Clackenbush?" the bicycle salesman squeaked. His Adam's apple was bouncing like a rubber ball.

"And, young man, be you acquainted with her?" Papa asked.

"Ah—oh—ah—well, no," Abe Brown sputtered.

Aunt Minnie dropped the cake server and stared at him. "Sure and 'tis a wonder you'd know her given name be Effie Mae," she said.

Before he could answer, Mama's soft voice broke into the discussion. I guess she figured we Conroys had been ill-mannered long enough. A guest must always be made to feel comfortable, and by the looks of ours he was anything but. "Shall we adjourn to the parlor * for some singing? Tommy and Susie will clear the table tonight," she said.

I finally got Tommy's attention. Before the others had a chance to get through the door, we had our heads together. We agreed that Abraham Lincoln Brown had more up his sleeve than his arm.

4
Rats Invade the Church

THE NEXT MORNING I arrived early at Wright's Drugstore to "work off my sentence." Sidney showed me how to sprinkle sawdust on the floorboards, then use a broom to pick up both sawdust and dirt.

I tried hard not to look at him and Sarah. Ugh! Every time he passed a mirror (the drugstore seemed full of them) he patted his hair and re-shaped his mustache. He'd pick imaginary lint off his trousers and smile over toward the lady's section where Sarah daintily flicked a dustcloth over bottles of Dr. Wilden's Quick Cure for Weak Women.

Sarah had given me a good tongue lashing last night. Afterward, I figured she and Sidney deserved each other. Her name may mean princess, but she acts like the Queen of Sheba. The only thing keeping her and Sidney from my full blessing, is the thought of Sidney as a brother.

About 10 A.M. our bicycle salesman walked in, carrying a long case. "Good morning, Mr. Wright," he said, and nearly tripped over my broom. He glared at me, then said to Sidney, "I was informed that you were in need of some new spokes for your damaged bicycle. And I can supply you with a superior type."

"Yes, I need some," Sidney answered, as he glanced at me.

I almost burst out with a sharp retort when I remembered that verse about waiting on God, so we won't be ashamed. I clamped my mouth shut and took out my anger on the floor. The dust simply flew.

"Achooo, achooo, aaaaacho!" Abe Brown sneezed so hard he bent over double.

"Susie, stop that!" Sidney ordered, as he grabbed the broom from me. "I told you it must be pushed slowly, so as not to stir up dust."

Being a "doer of the Word" isn't easy, I was learning.

* * *

Since it was prayer meeting night, Tommy and I walked over to the church early. (It's our job to fill the wall lamps with kerosene and light them.)

There are six windows with a lamp between each window. And there are six benches on each side of a center aisle. Up front, a raised platform holds the pulpit, an organ, and a few chairs. A heating stove sits in the back corner of the church.

From the outside our church looks like most of the western churches I've seen. It's just a box with a bell tower over the tacked-on entry room. There's a cellar underneath, but you enter it only from the outside. And the cellar fills with water early every spring when Muddy Creek overflows.

As soon as we opened the door, we could see that the late spring twilight coming in the windows had relieved us of our job.

Still, coming to service early wasn't a waste of time. Mrs. C always arrived early. That evening we watched her shuffle in with new respect. As usual, though, she passed us without speaking and sat down in her third row place.

"Wonder where she got that $50 gold piece?" Tommy whispered in my ear. We were leaning against the doorframe and staring at the back of her black bonnet.

"And how come a shifty-eyed stranger knew her name, but says he doesn't?" I asked in return.

Just then Abe Brown came in the outside door and I jabbed Tommy with my elbow.

Abe looked quickly around the building, then stooping over slightly, asked, "Would you carrot-tops mind introducing me to people?"

"As you can easily see, Mrs. Clackenbush is the only one here, so far," I retorted.

"That's fine," he answered.

So, I took him over to where she was sitting and, with my best manners, introduced them.

I'm sure the mystery would have been cleared up much earlier if I could have heard what he said to her. But there wasn't a chance. He stuck his long body between us, which left me looking at the back of his faded shirt and not hearing a word.

About then, the rest of the prayer meeting crowd began coming in.

Papa hurried up front and shuffled some papers around on the pulpit, while Abby started wheezing some notes out of the organ.

Mr. and Mrs. Joe Littleton, whom I secretly call Jack Spratt and his wife, came, with the Millers right on their heels. Sis Miller is my best friend, so I made a beeline over to join her.

As Sis and I settled down to catch up on the important events which had transpired since we'd been together on Sunday, the church filled quickly.

Papa signaled for Mama to take her seat, just as Sarah floated in on a cloud of eau de cologne with her hand on Sidney's arm. Just as she hoped, everyone stared. Papa had to announce the hymn number twice.

"It looks fatal," Sis whispered under cover of our hymnbook.

Everyone was as happy as Mrs. C's cats with a bowl of milk when Papa gave the news about the bell. He'd already ordered it from back East. It might arrive in a couple of months and would come by boat to The Dalles, then be freighted to Horseshoe Bend.

In our minds, I think, we all heard the deep tones of a bell ringing out over the countryside.

I sneaked a look at Mrs. C. She certainly didn't look like someone who'd made the purchase of a long-awaited bell possible. As usual, her face looked like a dried apple.

After giving the prayer requests and the praise due to God for our new bell, the men got together on the left and the women on the right side for prayer.

My bruised knees gave me fits when I knelt down beside the bench. Mrs. Littleton groaned and

moaned as she lowered her big bulk to the floor. I smelled Mrs. C somewhere close. Even Sarah's overpowering cologne couldn't drown out the smell of too many cats.

But the cat smell wasn't strong enough to keep away rats. I leaned my head against the bench seat and talked to God about my own problems while different ladies prayed for Grandma Miller's health and Sidney's uncle, who was home from Africa.

Suddenly something brushed my hair. I opened one eye in time to see a large, grayish-brown rat streak down the bench seat. It passed Nettie Fisher (who is husband-catching age) without her knowing it and ran smack into one of Mrs. Littleton's plump arms.

Her eyes flew open, then her mouth. Without making a sound, she slumped over between the benches and fell against Nettie Fisher. Nettie immediately started shrieking, "She's dead! She's dead!"

Bert Miller, Sis' big brother, and Mr. Smith, our schoolteacher, leaped over from the men's side. They somehow managed to get Mrs. Littleton out from between the benches and lay her on the seat.

Just as Mrs. Littleton was coming to, Joe reported the rat's escape down a hole into the cellar. Suggestions flew about as people discussed the best methods for ridding the church of rats. Besides nearly scaring a lady to death, they'd already damaged the hymnbooks and the carpet on the organ pedals.

With the help of smelling salts and Mr. Littleton's thin arm, Mrs. Littleton made it to their buggy. The excitement over, people began to drift toward home.

Everyone, that is, except Mr. Abe Brown and Mrs. C. While she sat placidly in her seat, he leaned over her talking at full gallop.

I grabbed Tommy. "Look at that, would you," I said. "How come he's got so much to tell Mrs. C if he doesn't even know her?"

Tommy was muttering to himself, his freckled nose wrinkled in thought: "Now if I prop the door up this way, it'll fall when the rat hits it—"

I'd lost Tommy again. He was inventing a rat trap to catch the church rats.

5 A Captive in the Trap

THE BICYCLE SALESMAN dashed out right after breakfast the next morning. I'd have given anything to be able to follow him. But I had my sweeping to do down at the drugstore. I guess I was reaping or "sweeping" what I'd sowed.

Tommy was too busy with his latest invention to follow a suspicious character.

Abe Brown didn't show up for noon dinner. And seeing Aunt Minnie sniff around, I knew she was put out. But I kind of enjoyed having a meal without that long-faced, sneaky-eyed salesman at the table.

"I'm planning to have my trap ready to set tonight," Tommy told Papa.

"Speaking of tonight," Sarah began, then turned pink and looked at her lap, "Sidney would like to speak to you, Papa."

"Sure an' I was thinkin' I had something he'd like," Papa said.

"What's that?" Joe piped up. "You're not giving him your telescope, be you?" Papa's telescope, which he lets us look through on special occasions, is the marvel of our household.

"An' I'm a wondering where that salesman be," Aunt Minnie worried as she got up and pushed some pans to the back of the stove. "The praties (she always uses the Irish name for potatoes) be cooling and him no more 'an a pile of bones. Selling bicycles—humph! Nobody'd buy one of them boneshakers, anyhow."

Nobody, but me, I sighed to myself, as I thought of all the obstacles between me and a bicycle.

"I still want to know—" Joe insisted.

"Now, Joseph, that's enough," Mama told him, as she tucked a stray hair behind her ear. "It's time you and Timmy took your naps. Susie will clear up since Aunt Minnie plans to get the rest of the garden in this afternoon. And that means you'll be helping in the garden, Tommy."

"I need to work on my trap," Tommy wailed.

Aunt Minnie turned from pouring water into the dishpan. "An' I'm sure that'll keep. 'Twill be all hands in the garden."

"Now Minnie," Papa protested. "I'm needin' to go see Jake Hummelmeister. 'Tis him that's having forty-eleven questions about the Scriptures."

Everyone scattered. Aunt Minnie and Abby dragged Tommy out to the garden, while Papa took off for the Hummelmeisters. Before Mama went to nap with the little boys, she and Sarah had a whispered talk about the evening. Afterward, Sarah sailed off to the drugstore.

I leaned against the washboard, soaking up the sunshine streaming through the red checked curtains. Slowly I swished hot, sudsy water across a plate. The sound of Aunt Minnie's voice floated in through the screen door and a couple of flies fussed to escape.

My head nodded, jerked, then nodded again as I glided out to Sis Miller's on a new royal blue lady's safety bicycle. In place of the usual one million ground squirrel holes, a path as smooth as a newly ironed sheet appeared under my tires.

"Achooo, achooo, aaaaacho!!"

I jumped, splashing soapy water down the front of my faded calico dress.

"God bless you," Aunt Minnie called, as the screen door banged behind her and the bicycle salesman.

He looked awful. His squinty eyes were swollen almost shut. The part that could be seen was runny and fiery red. His wheezy breaths came in gasps.

"Sure an' tis a sight you be," Aunt Minnie bellowed.

As if on signal, Mama hurried out of her bedroom. "Oh, my!" she murmured, as she clasped her hands together.

She lost no time in throwing a pinch of this and a spoonful of something else into a pan of water. Aunt Minnie stoked up the stove.* Together, they soon had a bitter smelling mixture bubbling on the stove.

Aunt Minnie shoved Abe Brown's nose into the steam. While he was breathing this brew, Mama went into her bedroom and came out with a can of her special asthmatic salve.

"An' what shenanigan brought on all this?" Aunt Minnie asked, while Mama laid a warm flannel cloth over the salve she'd smeared on his skinny chest.

"Cats," he gasped. "Every time I'm around them they stuff me up tighter than a fiddle string."*

Without thinking, I blurted out, "And what were you doing at Mrs. Clackenbush's all morning?"

"I'm a salesman you know," he sputtered before he went into another coughing fit.

Aunt Minnie sniffed. "Humph, an' 'twill be me, turned into a black-haired beauty, before Effie Mae buys a bicycle."

I agreed.

After supper, I helped Tommy carry the rattrap over to the church cellar.

First we had Papa inspect it.

Running his hands through his hair, until he looked like a red-headed porcupine, he asked, "An' why didn't anyone inform me 'twas bears over at the church?"

Tommy blushed. "I know the trap's kinda big, but the slats are close together, so a rat can't get out. See how the door's caught so it'll fall shut when they grab ahold of this piece of salt pork. Then there's no way for them to escape."

I thought the trap was clever, even if it was as big as a chicken crate. Papa *really* thought so too. He laughed and said he'd hate to be a church rat.

I dislike going down into our church cellar. But, Tommy had been loyal to me so many times, I couldn't refuse to help him carry the big awkward trap.

The stairs leading down to the cellar are on the outside. As soon as I put my foot on the first cool,

earth step, I felt a shiver start at my bare heel and crawl up to the back of my neck. Once I'd stepped on a lizard down here. Lizards, frogs, slugs, and spiders feel right at home in the damp and gloom.

Tommy pushed the door open and a cold rush of musty-smelling air hit us.

"Gloomy old place," Tommy commented, as he peered inside. We walked in with the trap and stood there, while our eyes adjusted to the dark. "I wonder where we should put it?" he said.

"Just set it anywhere," I urged, as I edged toward the door. The only thing the two small windows revealed was a pile of lumber. What bothered me was what that dim light *didn't* reveal.

Tommy put the box cage on the floor, then pushed the salt pork onto the prong of the stick that held the door up until a rat would grab the pork. After a final inspection, he followed me out of the cellar.

Just as he latched the door, Aunt Minnie yelled for him. He trotted across the yard, leaving me standing at the top of the cellar steps.

6 Sidney Takes the Fatal Step

I WAS SO glad to get out into the warm, friendly twilight, that I forgot my age and did several handsprings which landed me fairly close to the van.

I'd just started a debate with myself as to whether or not I should ask about Mr. Brown's health (and perhaps offer to help him sell bicycles while he recovered) when I heard the van door open. I stepped back into the shadows just as old long-and-skinny himself stepped out and hotfooted it toward town.

And here he'd retired after supper armed with more of Mama's asthmatic salve!

If only I had a bicycle, I thought. *Then catching up with him would be no trouble. The van should be full of them.* I headed toward the van.

But I stopped as I remembered the trouble I'd gotten into earlier in the week when I'd "borrowed" Sidney's bicycle. *So I'll run after him on my own two feet,* I decided. Running was one of my many unladylike accomplishments.

Before I could put this plan into action, Aunt Minnie bellowed, "Susie, 'tis you that be needed in this house."

"They probably want me to pass the betrothal* cake," I muttered to myself, as I shook the grass off my dress. Smoothing my flyaway hair, I went in the back door.

Aunt Minnie was in the kitchen stoking up the stove, while Abby served out gingerbread on plates. Over in the corner, Tommy scrubbed his hands in the washbasin.

"Bless me, but if this won't be the first wedding in the family," Aunt Minnie was saying. "Makes a body wish to be a mouse in the parlor corner and see what's going on in there."

"It seems like hours since Papa and Mama joined Sarah and Sidney in there," Abby answered. "I didn't know it took that long to ask for someone's hand in marriage."

"Well now, Abby, 'twill no doubt be your turn next," Aunt Minnie declared. "Since 'tis you that be only a year younger than Sarah."

Abby blushed, then said, "I doubt it. The fellows have never been attracted to me like they are to Sarah."

"Well now, don't 'judge a book by its cover,' I always say. And any man worth his salt better believe that too," Aunt Minnie said as she slapped the can of tea on the table.

I stood by the back door, just listening. The thought had never crossed my mind before, but Abby *was* plain. She was so kindhearted that I'd never noticed what she looked like. Could she be worried that she might end up an "old maid" like Aunt Minnie?

Her next comment answered that question. "There are certainly worse things than not marrying," she said. "Think of how many things a single lady can do for the Lord."

"Bless me, but if that isn't so!" Aunt Minnie exclaimed. Then she turned around and saw me. "Susie, you get to whipping that cream to put on the gingerbread."

With Tommy spelling me off on the eggbeater, we beat the cream to soft peaks.

Still, the parlor door stayed closed.

"Maybe Papa is marrying them right now," I suggested. "Seems every time a person turns around, some couple is getting hitched in there."

Just then the parlor door opened, and Mama came into the kitchen to see if the refreshments were ready.

Abby served the tea, while Tommy and Aunt Minnie passed the gingerbread around. I followed them with the tray of silverware, cream, and sugar.

The parlor seemed stiff and cold after the warm, cozy kitchen. Sarah sat primly on one side of the horsehair sofa, while Sidney, in his best suit, perched uncomfortably on the other end.

Mama smiled and rocked her chair a little, while Papa boomed out, "Sidney, 'tis this way, I'll be having you to know. My daughters, all three of them, are mighty special to me, and I'll not be giving them away to just anyone."

Sidney squirmed, ran his finger under his collar, and looked like he might make a dash for the door any minute.

Then, Papa lowered his voice and his next words had a little tremble in them. "But I'm certain that it's you, Sidney, that will take good care of my Sarah."

On Abby's way back to the kitchen, Papa caught her hand and said, "And you be my fair colleen."

I nearly spilled the cream off my tray when Papa added, "And 'tis Susie that be the joy of my heart."

It seemed that in spite of stolen bicycles, Papa included me as one of his special daughters. I could have done a handspring right in the parlor!

Until I served Sarah, that is.

While Papa was still informing Sidney about the marvels of his daughters, Sarah grabbed the skirt of my dress and hissed, "Susie, how did you ever get this grass stain on your dress? And your braids have grass sticking out of them. How could you look like a scarecrow on such an important occasion!"

I yanked my dress from her hand and nearly upset her teacup. If it hadn't been for Papa and Mama, I would have told her exactly what I thought of her snippity ways—and her future husband's too.

Instead, I sailed out of the parlor, my warm bubbly feeling turned to anger.

I'd intended to slam the tray on the kitchen table and stomp off to bed. But Abby and Aunt Minnie were in the kitchen washing up and harmonizing on the hymn, "Nearer, My God to Thee"—

"E'en though it be a cross that raiseth me;
Still all my song shall be,

Nearer my God, to Thee,
Nearer, my God, to Thee, Nearer to Thee!"

Those words pulled me up short. I crept off to bed, remembering Jesus' patience with me and with those who hated Him and finally put Him to death on a cross.

* * *

Naturally, Tommy and I hurried over to the church cellar to inspect his trap first thing the next morning. What wasn't natural was the captive we found in it. Not an ugly old rat but a snarling tiger cat.

"I wonder how that cat got in here?" Tommy said as he inspected the walls for possible holes.

"I'm sure it's Mrs. C's old fighting tiger!" I declared. "He fights every cat in town. And she's the only person he'll get near. Why, Miss Johnson said—"

"Let's get him out of here," Tommy said, interrupting my report.

It was easy. The minute Tommy lifted the cage door the cat shot out of the cellar as though a pack of hounds were on his tail.

"Guess he doesn't like this place any better than I do," I said, as I peered suspiciously at a dark spot on the floor that looked like a lizard.

"I know I closed and fastened the door last night," Tommy reassured himself, as he reset his trap. "How'd a cat get in here, anyway?"

"Since cats and the bicycle salesman don't get along, I guess we can't blame him for the cat being here," I said. I was sorry I couldn't blame something on Abe Brown.

"But, *someone* had to let that cat in here," Tommy said. "I wonder who?"

7
A Light in the Cellar

AS SOON AS we all gathered around the table for supper that evening, Papa cleared his throat. "Sure an' tis a lot we have to thank God for tonight," he declared. "If gettin' a God-fearing young man for a son-in-law isn't enough to make a man's heart sing."

Then he led us in singing, "Praise God, from Whom all Blessings Flow." Meanwhile the smell of Aunt Minnie's Irish stew wrapped itself around my nose.

Sidney a blessing? I guessed his uppity ways bothered only me. Maybe if I waited long enough, they'd get less important. I rubbed my leg against Sniffer's silky fur and sighed. It seemed as if life was one long string of waiting.

After praying, Papa delivered some more news. It snapped me out of the dismals, double-quick.

Mrs. Wright's brother—Sidney's uncle—was a missionary to Africa. He was in town and would be showing magic lantern slides of Africa tomorrow night at church!

It's amazing the noise 10 people—except for one silent bicycle salesman—can make when they all talk at once. Mama's rule, "children should be seen, not heard," went out the back door with Sniffer. (Noise hurt Sniffer's ears. I'm sure no one but me heard the screen door bang as he left.)

"I hope there's lions in the pictures," said Joe.

"And headhunters," Tommy declared.

"Not a chance. They'd never show naked people in church," I said.

Abe Brown continued to eat. Just looking at his long, sour face, a person would never guess we'd just had such big news. Why, a missionary was the most exciting person to come to Horseshoe Bend since the Snake Doctor!*

To get our attention, Papa struck the edge of his cup with his knife. "We've only tonight and tomorrow to spread the news," he said.

Getting last minute church news out involves the whole family. Papa delivers the information to the outlying ranches on horseback. Tommy and I spread the news to the people in Horseshoe Bend, on foot. Meanwhile, Mama, using her best lettering, makes signs for Abby and Sarah to put up in the stores and hotel. Aunt Minnie directs operations.

"I could cover my territory in half the time if I had a bicycle to ride," I blurted out to Mr. Brown.

He stopped shoveling stew into his mouth a moment and glared at me through those squinty little eyes of his. I looked down at my empty plate just as Aunt Minnie said, "Sure an' aren't you the one that looked the beggar-maid not so many days past, all on account of a boneshaker?"

"I wouldn't need to go down any hills. Riding on the level is as easy as falling off a log—" I stopped abruptly. The comparison wasn't too good.

"That's enough, Susie," Mama said. Her quiet voice carried over the noise Aunt Minnie made stacking plates. "If you walk quickly, I'm sure you can make it home by dark."

"Sure an' Susie can take the north end of town, startin' with Mrs. Clackenbush. Tommy'll do the south side," Papa directed.

Later, as I hurried toward Mrs. C's house, Fred-

die Johnson glided past me. He *couldn't* be, but he
was! He was riding a new shiny black bicycle!
Maybe Mr. Brown *had* made a sale. I caught my
breath as the setting sun flashed off the nickle-
plated spokes and made the enameled frame shine
like polished glass. Freddie grinned at me and for
a moment rode "no-hands."

The "green-eyed monster" grabbed me somewhere close to my heart. It wasn't fair! His father
ran a prosperous livery stable, so he could sail
around town on a bicycle. But because we lived
mostly off church offerings, I had to trudge along
on foot. The warm evening breeze carried frogs'
chug-a-rums from Muddy Creek. They sounded to
me as if they were croaking, "Too bad; too bad;
too bad."

When I got to Mrs. C's, I almost stepped on a
cat. It was curled up on the big flat rock in front
of the door. I knocked several times before Mrs. C
lifted the dark cloth hanging over her window and
peered out. I stepped back and looked at the house.
The logs seemed to hug the ground as if they were
hiding something.

Finally, she opened the door a crack.

"Hello, Mrs. Clackenbush. I came by to tell you
that Mr. Jackman is in town. He's Mrs. Wright's
brother—a missionary from Africa. He's going to

show his magic lantern slides of Africa at the church tomorrow night at 8 o'clock."

She opened the door a little wider. A cat squeezed out along with an unpleasant odor.

"Thank you," Mrs. C said. Then more to herself, she mumbled, "Expect he could use some money."

"Well, I guess so! You show me a preacher or a missionary who can't!" I declared.

Her eyes popped open and she drew back into her house. Without another word, she closed the door and bolted it in my face.

Everyone else I called on thought my news was great.

Ten thousand steps and two and one half hours later, I plodded into our backyard. Some noise on the church side of the yard caused me to lift my chin off my chest.

"Wowee, what is that light doing in the church cellar!" I exclaimed to myself. I could see a dim light showing through the two cellar windows.

I forgot all about tired feet and took off like a lightning streak.

Thud! Next thing I knew I was stretched out flat—sprawled across Sarah and Sidney's laps!

Sarah recovered first. "Susanne Conroy, what do you mean by this? Haven't you any pride? I'd be ashamed—well, get up!"

I slowly pushed my face off the grass and pulled my legs off Sidney's lap. I yanked my skirts around as I rolled over beside Sarah. How embarrassing! Then I remembered the reason I'd been in such a rush.

"There's a light in the church cellar!" I yelled.

But when the three of us looked in that direction, the church was just a dark outline against a star-speckled sky.

"Don't be ridiculous, Susie, who'd be in the church cellar this time of night. And if you don't start acting your age, think how disappointed Mama'll be—"

That did it! No one knew how much I wanted to please Mama. I'd had enough of Sarah's lectures. I hopped to my feet and shot back, "Just what are *you two* doing out here, anyway? Sitting in the middle of a dark yard, with your legs stuck out, so anyone crossing the yard could trip over you."

Sarah's tone changed from angry to honey-sweet. "Sidney's giving me lessons in astronomy," she said.

With one backward glance at the church, I headed toward our house. My ripped skirt was dragging. I'd failed God and Mama *again*. I hadn't *waited* and I was *ashamed*. At least old Sidney had kept his mouth shut.

I met Tommy at the back door and asked if he'd checked on his trap tonight.

"Nope, I'm just now getting home," he said.

I told him about the light in the church, and we both looked over at it.

"Are you sure you saw a light?" he asked me as he opened the door.

"Yes, I know I did," I said. "And I've never known a rat to carry a lantern." I let the door slam behind me.

8 On the Trail of an Intruder

TOMMY AND I inspected the cellar on Saturday morning. But we found nothing. Not even a cat— or a rat.

"Let's make a cage to catch whoever's snooping around down here," I suggested to Tommy, as he closed the cellar door.

"How?" he asked.

"Well, we could do like they do in Africa," I said, remembering the pictures we'd seen the last time a missionary came. "We could dig a big hole and cover it with brush. Then whoever came in the basement would fall through as they walked in."

60

"But what's to keep them from climbing out?" Tommy, the practical one, said.

"Guess that is a poor idea," I admitted. "Then how about putting some string here across the basement steps and tripping him."

"What happens after he's tripped?" Tommy asked, as he locked the door and we walked slowly up the dirt steps.

I thought a minute. "We could tie that old cowbell to the string. It would ring when he hit the string. Then we could come running and catch him flat-footed."

Tommy looked skeptical. "You're sure you saw lights down there last night?" he asked.

"I *know* I saw lights," I declared. "And that means someone was there last night and the night before too. Someone had to let Mrs. C's tiger cat in. I bet it was that sneaky salesman, even if cats do fuss him up."

"I can't see what he'd want down there," Tommy said. We both looked back down the cellar steps.

"That's why we've got to catch him," I said.

"I'm not sure this'll work," Tommy said slowly. "But I'll fasten some twine down close to that second step so nobody'll notice it. And I'll put sleigh bells on it. Nobody'd hear one clunk from a cowbell. There's some twine in the kitchen and—"

"OK, that sounds like it might work," I said. "I've got to get over to the drugstore now to clean."

So Tommy hurried away to carry out our plans and I smiled to myself all the way to the drugstore. Anyone nosing around the cellar tonight would be sorry!

By 8 o'clock that evening the church was packed. Close to the front of the middle aisle stood Aunt Minnie's bedside table. On it sat a big five-sided black box with what looked like a chimney sprouting from the top.

Excitement ran through the crowd like an eastern Oregon windstorm. Of course the grown-ups acted as if magic lantern slides were everyday stuff. But their excited whispers gave them away.

We kids were wound up tighter than a dollar watch. We didn't care who knew it.

Joe hopped from seat to seat. Tommy eyed the black machine as closely as possible without actually touching it. Freddie Johnson crossed his eyes at Sis Miller and me. Even Nettie Fisher fidgeted a lot—until Bert Miller slid in beside her.

Timmy was sitting on my lap, so as not to miss anything. He fussed and squirmed. Finally I realized that he needed to visit the little house out back.* Wouldn't you know! Disgusted, I pulled him out so fast his baby legs flew out behind him.

On the way back, we slowed down enough for me to catch my breath. The strains of "The Call to Reapers" drifted out the door. They had begun the service. At least Mr. Jackman wasn't showing his pictures yet. I glanced at the cellar steps, then bent over and looked again. The rope and bells were in place, ready for our church prowler.

Mr. and Mrs. Jackman sang for us in Swahili, an African language. They chose "O Happy Day." They seemed like just ordinary people. Mrs. Jackman fluttered a lace-trimmed hanky around just as daintily as Mama. Mr. Jackman was dressed like Papa and had a bald head.

We teetered on the edges of our seats, eagerly waiting to see the pictures. But Mr. Jackman proceeded to explain that the contraption in the middle of the room was a polyopticon.* It really wasn't magic, just marvelous. He used it instead of a magic lantern because he made his own pictures. He didn't use ready-made slides. This machine enlarged his pictures 400 times!

He was just warming up to his subject, it turned out. He picked up his camera and started explaining about that too. I thought I'd pop if he didn't get on with the pictures! But Tommy hung on every word. I figured Tommy would try to make a camera next.

But the wait was worth it. After Mr. Jackman lit the lamp in the black box, he opened a little door and put a picture in. That picture appeared as if by magic on Mama's bed sheet, tacked up in front. It was just as if God had picked us up and set us down on a jungle path.

There weren't any headhunter pictures. But Mr. Jackman did show pictures of snakes, dead tigers, grass huts, and black people. He showed other scenes of jungle with monkeys and bright colored birds. A person could almost hear the birds squawking and monkeys screeching in all that underbrush. Missionary Jackman told us that the people who lived there and walked those jungle paths had many of the same problems we had. Jesus' death and resurrection took care of their sins the same as ours.

I gazed at a girl whose dress was a colorful cloth wrapped around her. *Does she act first and think afterwards like I do?* I wondered.

Imagine my joy when I saw Mrs. Jackman pictured up there on the sheet, on a *bicycle!* And she was a *lady missionary* no less.

"Wowee!" I blurted out loud. Sis jabbed me in the ribs as Sarah leaned over the seat and thumped me on the head.

To my delight, Mr. Jackman showed us two more

pictures of themselves on bicycles. He explained that they could cover the miles on two wheels much faster than on two feet.

I hoped the Conroy household had heeded that! All too soon, Mr. Jackman blew out the flame in his black box. The room was as dark and empty as a big barrel.

Then Papa tromped up front and Mr. Littleton lit the church lamps. Just like that, the jungle paths disappeared. We were eastern Oregonians again, sitting on Horseshoe Bend Community Church benches.

Papa asked Mr. Littleton and Mr. Miller to come up and take the collection for the missionaries. A noise in back made me turn around then. And I just happened to see our bicycle salesman slip out the church door.

As soon as Papa announced the benediction, I took off for the door too. I felt like old Sniffer must when he's out on a jackrabbit's trail!

I was making good headway through the crowd blocking the door when Mrs. Littleton chose to go out the same moment I did. I bumped smack into her huge posterior, but it didn't affect her any more than a gnat would if it flew into me. But Mama, who was standing in her usual greeting-the-people place, noticed. She reached out and grabbed me.

So instead of trailing a top suspect, I had to stand beside her, as if I were a two-year-old.

The next morning was Sunday, and the sun, streaming in my window, awoke me. For some reason, I felt as low as a puddle. I burrowed down into my bedding, unable to think of one thing worth getting up for. The magic lantern show was over. My chances of getting a bicycle were growing dimmer by the day. And I was sure I'd never become a genteel lady.

"Psst, Susie."

I peeked out from under the sheet to see Tommy's freckled face poking around the bedroom door.

"Did you hear the bells last night?" he asked as he came into the room.

"What bells?" I asked, groggily.

"The ones we tied to the cellar steps," he said.

"No, did you?"

"No, but Mr. Brown just limped into the kitchen with a big bruise on the side of his face," Tommy told me.

"Wowee! That settles it, Tommy!" I exclaimed, as I began to get out of bed. "Give me a chance to get dressed. I'm going right down there and accuse him before the whole family. He can't weasel out of this one."

Tommy shoved me back down into a sitting position. "And what are you going to accuse him of?" he asked.

"Of snooping around the cellar, of course," I said. "And bothering Mrs. C, and not letting me look in his van. And—not showing his bicycles and—"

"But what's wrong with any of those things, Susie?" Tommy said. "Nothing! Absolutely nothing! You'd just get into more hot water for spouting off."

"You're right," I answered, deflated. "And here I promised God after last night that I'd learn to wait. Guess He sent you along to help me keep my promise."

"That's it. We'll have to wait and watch. Act like we don't know a thing. That's the only way we'll be able to find out what he's up to," Tommy said as he left the room.

"See you at breakfast," I called to him. I dug my Bible out from under my pillow and opened it to read as I tried to do each day.

9
Mrs. C Reveals Her Secret

DUST PARTICLES floated lazily in the wedge of morning sunlight coming through the drugstore's big front window. I felt as light and free as the dust I was stirring up. It had been almost a week since my famous bicycle accident. I seemed to be healed inside and out. Even waiting for Abe Brown to make a false move didn't seem so tedious this morning. *Curious*, I thought, *how listening to and obeying God's Word could do that.*

Merrily I sang a new song Abby had just taught us and swept as I sang. She'd heard the song over at the hotel, then picked the tune out on our parlor

68

organ. I guess it appealed to me because it was about bicycle riding:

Daisy, Daisy,
Give me your answer, do.
I'm half crazy all for the love of you.

I swung the broom around the corner of the crutches and shoulder brace shelf, as I sang the words.

It won't be a stylish marriage;
I can't afford a carriage,
But you'll look sweet
Upon the seat of a bicycle built for two-o-o-o.

Holding the last note, I swooshed the broom down the center aisle. Then I pulled it back toward me and leaning on its handle, I closed my eyes and inhaled deeply.

The delicious smell of the drugstore rushed in on me. By themselves, sweet-smelling cough syrup, fishy-smelling cod liver oil, and flowery-smelling perfumed soap aren't much. But put them under the same roof with the bitter odor of medicines, Sidney's strong-scented hair oil, and the wicked aroma of tobacco, and the results are powerful.

Bang!

The front door flew open and one wheezing bicycle salesman rushed in. "Mr. Wright, say Mr. Wright—achoo—a-a-ah! W-where's the doctor? I can't find him no place."

Sidney came dashing out of the back room and grabbed Abe Brown by the arm. "Calm down, Mr. Brown. Where are you hurt?" He looked Abe up and down. "Outside of that gasping you look all right to me."

"It's not me—a-a-ach-choo! It's Effie Mae Clackenbush. She might be dead. Achoo."

I gripped the broom handle till my fingers hurt.

Sidney took the news calmly. He led Mr. Brown over to a chair where the customers sit while waiting for Mr. Wright to prepare their medicine. Then he gave him a whiff of something out of a bottle, before answering him. "Now tell me exactly what's wrong with Mrs. Clackenbush."

"When I got there this morning, she didn't answer her door."

Sidney raised his eyebrows slightly.

"I had an appointment with her, so I knew she should be there. She only has one door and two windows. They were all locked, so I broke into the back window. Achoo! How about another sniff of that stuff? She must have a million cats in that

place. A-a-achoo! And there she was on the floor.
And that doctor's not to home."

Abe Brown's Adam's apple started slipping, and
he looked like he could use a bottle of Dr. Row-
land's nerve pills in the worst way. "She could be
dying!" he yelled as he shot out of the chair. "Then
my goose would be cooked."*

*What an odd stick,** I thought, as I pushed my
chin down on the top of the broom handle.

"The doctor is out fixing the Webster boy's leg.
That's a little ways out of town," Sidney told him.
Then he turned to where I stood, still clutching
the broom handle. "Susie, I can't leave the store
since my father's gone and Sarah hasn't come yet.
You get my bicycle out back and ride out and get
the doctor. Hurry!"

I came to life and made for the door before
Sidney could change his mind. As I dashed out, I
heard him telling Mr. Brown how to care for Mrs.
C until the doctor got there.

I pushed the bicycle along until I was beside the
drugstore's raised porch. From the porch, I climbed
easily onto the bicycle, gave myself a shove, and
wobbled off down the street. I nearly crashed at
the corner of Main and Third when a barking dog
rushed at me.

By the time I passed Sarah, mincing toward the

drugstore, I had the bicycle under control. She stopped and stared at me as if I were a freak from a sideshow. Finding her voice, she screeched, "Susie Conroy, you get back to the store with Sidney's bicycle!"

I carefully pedaled on, realizing there was no time to explain things to her. Sidney could do it much better.

My ride to the Webster's taught me one thing at least: You can't trust advertising. There was a lot more to riding a bicycle than "straddle a saddle then paddle and skedaddle."* (That's what the ad had said in the "The Cycle" magazine.)

By the time I turned off the bumpy road, I felt as if I'd ruined my liver and knew I had torn my new lace drawers. I half fell off the bicycle at the Webster's lane. My legs felt all wobbly as I pushed Sidney's bicycle the rest of the way to the house.

Doc had his buggy, and I gladly accepted his offer to ride back to town with him. He put Sidney's bicycle in and I gingerly lowered my sore self onto the seat.

The buggy springs groaned as Doc plopped his big frame on the seat and lightly spanked the reins on his horse's back. We whizzed along and he chanted:

"Whoopee! Out of the way!
We come with lightning speed:
There's nothing like the rattling gait *
Of the flying velocipede.*

"Doc, have you ridden a bicycle?" I asked in surprise.

"Nope, never intend to, either," he declared.

"Do you think they're bad for a person's health?" I asked, a bit worried.

"Nope, very healthful exercise," he said. "You'll toughen up soon."

I thought he must know about my sore backside, but I only said, "I doubt if I'll get the chance. Sidney Wright's only letting me use his bicycle because of this emergency. The last chuckhole sort of did me in. But your song is right, I made it out here with lightning speed on the flying velocipede."

" 'Tain't my song. Read it somewhere in a medical journal. It said cycling builds up feeble frames and drives away sciatica, headaches, insomnia, and dyspepsia."*

"Wowee! Would you be willing to tell my family that?" I asked as we halted in front of Mrs. C's cabin.

Doc jumped out of the buggy with amazing agility and headed for the door. "You tell 'em yourself,

Susie. You're the one with the gift of gab,"* he called back, just as Abe Brown stuck his head out the door.

Abe took off as soon as Doc went in. I figured he was on his way to our house. He sure needed doctoring after being in that cat-infested place.

I slipped in the door along with a calico cat. The house smelled worse than a pigsty and was as dark as the church cellar. I stayed beside the door, curious as to what would happen next.

Doc picked up Mrs. C and laid her on top of her table. When she groaned, I realized she was alive at least. Doc found a lamp, then set it on the stove top where it cast a warm glow over the table. Then, he began his examination. As he pressed and poked, he murmured soothing words, so as not to upset the patient.

Laid out on the table like that, Mrs. C looked as small and helpless as a worn-out rag doll. She moaned and groaned, while Doc mumbled something about her hip.

About then, her little black eyes popped open and she tensed in alarm.

"Now, Mrs. Clackenbush, it's just old Doc. I'm here to help you. Don't be frightened."

"Doctors cost money," she said as clear as a church bell.

"Now don't you worry about money," he said. "You just set your mind on getting well."

"Doctor, my money's under them boards in the church cellar," she added.

"Yes, yes," Doc mumbled as he moved her leg.

"Ah-h-h, under the boards, mind you—" she murmured as she closed her eyes.

My heart did a flip. Did I hear right? Could it be true? If it was, it answered a lot of questions. Doc thought her mind was wandering. But he hadn't seen the light in the church cellar when no one should be down there. And he hadn't released one of Mrs. C's cats from a rattrap!

The cat could have followed Mrs C into the church cellar. And the light I'd seen must have come from Mrs. C's lantern when she'd been down there getting money to give to the missionary. I was itching to share the news with Tommy. But first I had to check out that cellar!

Doc was so absorbed in his work that I'm sure he never knew when I came in or when I dashed out. I pulled Sidney's bicycle off the buggy and pedaled toward the church as if a prairie fire were at my back.

10
Trapped in the Cellar

AFTERWARD, I could never recall my ride to the church. If my muscles rebelled, I wasn't aware of it. My thoughts were on one thing: money in the church cellar!

The cold dampness that met me when I flung the cellar door open revived my brain enough for me to realize I'd need a light to do any searching.

I scrambled up the church steps to borrow a lamp. By the time I'd found a match and hopped back down to the cellar, I was breathless. My fingers trembled as I lit the lamp.

Holding the light high and forgetting all about

the creepy creatures that lived there, I circled the pile of boards. I saw nothing unusual. Then I crouched down and duck-walked around them. My legs reminded me that they'd been treated badly enough today, just as I spied the sack.

It was an ordinary flour sack pushed between two boards close to the floor.

The contents rattled when I picked it up. Painful prickles stabbed my legs as I straightened up. My bicycle ride accounted for them, but the bag in my hand was responsible for the way the lamp shook.

I set the lamp on top of the boards so I could spread the top of the sack open.

"So you found it!" Abe Brown snarled, as he suddenly loomed over me.

Startled, I instinctively stuck the bag behind me.

"You might as well give it here, carrottop. I'll get it one way or another," he said.

I looked up into his narrowed eyes, still red and runny from his encounter with Mrs. C's cats. *He isn't fooling,* I thought.

I'd never been so scared in my life. Having the Miller's bull chase me hadn't been this bad. There'd been the fence ahead with Sis behind it, cheering me on to safety.

But today I was alone, except for Abe. His heavy

breathing seemed to fill this thick-walled cellar.

When he grabbed my arm, cold shivers jumped around inside me, causing the gold pieces to rattle.

"Are you going to give that to me without any fuss?" he wheezed, as he began tugging on my arm. "Or do I have to force it from you. There's no one to help you, so you'd better give it here, or you'll be sorry."

If Abe hadn't told me I had no one to help me, I might never have remembered a Bible verse I'd learned the past year: "Be not afraid, neither be dismayed, for the Lord thy God is with thee whithersoever thou goest" (Joshua 1:9). That meant I *wasn't* alone. God was down in this dark hole with me!

Remembering that gave me the courage to start talking normally. "This happens to belong to Mrs. Clackenbush," I said. "Why she left it here, I can't imagine. But I mean to see that she gets it back. I'd think you'd be ashamed of yourself, trying to steal a sick old woman's money."

I gave him a look that should have shamed a king. But he didn't look ashamed and he didn't let go of my arm. I began backing around the boards, talking all the time. "How can you be so heartless?" I asked.

"Oh, shut your mouth," he spit out, making me

feel even more like a rat with a cat on its tail.

"How can you say that?" I demanded.

"It was my uncle that willed it to her. But I'm the one that had to live with the beast. Him a-beatin' and a-knockin' me around ever since I could walk. How do you think he made all that money if it wasn't by making me a slave on that farm. I earned every penny of it and then some."

"Just what does *your* uncle have to do with Mrs. C?" I asked.

"He was her brother. When he died, do you think he left me a penny? No!" he yelled, as if the awful reality seemed to sink in again.

I began to plan as I continued creeping around the boards. I'd stall him off until I had a straight run for the door. "Maybe she'd share some of it," I said. "It feels like quite a bit."

"Share it! With that horrible old witch?" he cried. "She's going to give it all to *God*, she says. Won't trust a bank. She had it all turned into gold pieces to throw away on mealymouthed goody-goodies."

Abe Brown's mouth started working and his Adam's apple bouncing. I knew then how a rat must feel when the cat's got his paw on the rat's tail. It was time I left.

Catching him unaware, I jerked free and sprinted

for the door. Abe lunged at me. But he started sneezing and tripped over a board that stuck out further than the others in the stack. On his way down, he hit his head on the corner of Tommy's rattrap.

I looked back and saw that he seemed stunned. Instead of doing the sensible thing and high-tailing * it out of the cellar, I dropped the sack, grabbed the rope that Tommy'd used for tripping purposes, and tied Abe's wrists together.

The knots weren't anything to brag about, but either the rope around his wrists or the bang on the head seemed to calm him down. As I looked down at his long, skinny form stretched out on the dirt, he started wheedling.

"Now, look, Susie, I'll tell you what I'll do. There must be about $1,000 in that bag. I'll leave enough for Aunt Effie Mae to live on and feed all the cats in the country. And I'll give you plenty, so you can buy the best bicycle made, since unfortunately there aren't any in my van. I'll even give you enough to buy one for your friend, so you two can ride together.

"Then I'll take the rest and leave. You keep your mouth shut about the whole thing, and no one will be the wiser. Everyone knows Aunt Effie Mae is a might touched, so they'll not pay any mind to what she says. You can tell people she bought the bicycles."

His sudden change of direction left me speechless.

"If you'd seen how hard I had to work on that farm back in Missouri," he continued, "ever since my ma died. He made me a slave. Never a kind word to me, nor anyone else. Whippin' me whenever it crossed his mind. Then just before he died, he up and sold everything and left it all to a sister he hadn't seen for a coon's age.* Now does that sound fair?"

"No, but maybe she'd share if you explained it all to her," I suggested, with something close to sympathy.

"Ha, that's what I did!" he exclaimed as he sat up. "Why'd you think I came all the way to this back-of-beyond place, pretending to be a bicycle salesman? Knowing she was the churchy type, I looked up the preacher and found out where she lived. And I've talked to her every which way. Still, she says I'm a godless man and so was my uncle. She's making sure the money'll be spent for God now. She says I can make my own way in life."

"No wonder she hid the money down here, with you a-pestering her," I said.

Abe must have sensed my weakening, for he

started talking, nonstop. He pictured my bicycle and Effie Mae happy with plenty and him getting what rightfully belonged to him.

I hesitated, while my thoughts chased each other around. I'd never get a bicycle any other way. And Mrs. C didn't seem to have much respect for money. (Imagine her putting it in a bag in a church cellar!) And it did seem as if Abe had earned part of the money, anyway.

But, on the other hand, that money wasn't really his to do with as he liked. "Thou shalt not steal" and "thou shalt not lie" were Bible verses I'd learned when I was Timmy-size. Following Abe's plan, meant turning a deaf ear to the Lord.

"No, Mr. Brown, your plan isn't right. Everything about it's against the Bible," I told him, as I picked up the sack.

"What d'ya mean? I earned it!" he screeched, as he jumped up and, turning pale, wrenched his hands free of the rope.

"It would be stealing and lying, as you'd well know if you ever read the Bible," I yelled over my shoulder as I took off around the rattrap and fled out the door, smack into Tommy.

"You little rascal!" Abe screamed. "I'll wring your neck as soon as—ahhhh, ugh!"

This time Abe had stumbled over the rattrap.

Evidently, he was so mad he couldn't see straight. Tommy shoved me aside and disappeared into the cellar. I followed him back inside.

Abe was draped over the large cage, when Tommy leaped on his back and knocked the wind out of him. Tommy clung like a burr on a dog's back, while Abe struggled to get his wind.

"Susie, don't stand there with your mouth hanging open. Help me!"

Dropping the flour sack, I hopped on behind Tommy, just as Abe got his breath and started hollering words too horrible to print.

His rage frightened me worse than any of his other moods. I shuddered to think of what he'd do after he flipped us off his back.

11 A Bicycle in the Family

"SURE AN' WHAT shenanigans be goin' on here? You're yellin' loud enough to be heard in the next county." Papa's voice boomed in through the cellar door.

"Papa!" Tommy and I cried in unison, as we jumped off Abe's back and ran joyfully to meet Papa.

Remembering the sack of coins, I did a quick about-face and snatched the bag off the ground.

"Look at this bag full of gold, Papa," I gasped, holding the sack out to him. "This is Mrs. C's inheritance. And he," I turned and pointed at Abe who was slowly lifting himself off the rattrap, "was going to steal it."

Papa ran his fingers through his hair. "An' is that the truth?" he asked, walking over to Abe.

He took hold of Abe Brown's arm and led him up the cellar steps. I figured Abe might run for it, but his bravado all melted away, like a chunk of ice in the sunlight.

He looked like a scarecrow with his straw-colored hair sticking out every which way and his clothes all messed up. He hung his head sheepishly as Papa began questioning me about the contents of the flour sack.

As I launched into the exciting events that had just befallen me, Sniffer announced the arrival of Doc's buggy.

The kitchen window flipped up and Aunt Minnie stuck her head out to see who was coming. In no time at all, she and Mama rushed out on the front porch.

"Say, Brother Conroy," Doc called, "come give me a hand with Effie Mae."

Abe stared at the ground, as he followed Papa over to the buggy.

"You can give us a hand here too, young man," Doc told Abe.

Doc, Abe, and Papa handled Mrs. C as if she

were a porcelain doll, carrying her carefully into the house.

We all crowded into Aunt Minnie's bedroom, as they installed her in Aunt Minnie's bed. Doc told Papa and Mama that she had fallen at home and broken her hip. At her age it would be a long time before she could do for herself.

I guess he knew he'd brought her to the right place with Mama murmuring "poor dear" and Aunt Minnie fussing around with the bedclothes.

After Doc gave Mrs. C some relaxing powders, the rest of us—Papa, Tommy, Mama, Abe, Doc, and me—gathered around the table as if by command.

Aunt Minnie whipped around, pouring coffee, while Abby whacked off big hunks of chocolate cake.

Sidney and Sarah arrived, full of questions about Mrs. C's condition. Sidney perched on the upended kindling box since all the chairs, but Aunt Minnie's and Abby's, were occupied. (Sidney is too much of a gentleman to take a lady's seat.) I hoped he'd get a splinter in his worsted trousers!

I'd plopped down, still clutching the bag of gold, and stuck my feet on top of Sniffer, before I realized how dog-tired I was.

Papa cleared his throat and looked around the

group before he spoke. "Sure and 'tis me Susie who's uncovered some mighty strange doings today."

I felt uncomfortably warm as everyone but Abe looked at me. Abe had slumped over and sat staring at the tablecloth. His face was as white and blank as his plate.

"Now, Susie, we're waiting," Papa prompted.

That's all it took for me to start talking full gallop.

"Sure and 'tis past believing," Papa commented as I told about Abe being kin to Effie Mae.

After I'd described Abe's mean uncle, Doc said, "Instability must run in the family."

"Bless me, if they aren't odd ducks," Aunt Minnie added.

But, Mama patted Abe on the arm and said, "Poor boy, never to have had a family to love him and lead him to God."

"My, a bicycle does seem to have been useful today," Sarah agreed when I told about being sent after Doc.

The words tumbled out and I waved my arms wildly for emphasis when I came to the "great discovery" and my "near capture" and Tommy's rescue.

"The Lord preserve us!" Aunt Minnie exclaimed.

"Seems as if Tommy's trap caught a bigger rat than he expected," Doc said, laughing.

With all the interruptions, the clock had struck two before I ended my story. As soon as I finished, everyone began talking at once.

"Susie, sounds like you looked before you leaped this time," Abby said.

And Mama smiled approvingly. "Yes, dear, I believe you are beginning to see the advantages of waiting on the Lord before acting," she said.

"The whole thing sounds like a penny thriller!"* Tommy exclaimed.

"Sure and who'd be reading them trashy things?" Aunt Minnie said, looking suspiciously at Tommy.

Doc rattled the dishes as he pounded on the table for order. "Seems to me, we'd best get this gold down to Fisher at the bank, first thing, so's no one else is tempted to make off with it."

I handed the sack to him, relieved to have it in good hands.

Papa turned to Abe, who scrooched* lower in his chair. "And me young friend, what might you be planning to do now?" he asked kindly.

Handling kindness seemed hard for Abe. His Adam's apple jumped around a bit, as he toyed with his fork. He didn't meet Papa's look, and muttered something about "not being sure."

"Sure an' I'm a-thinkin' he ought to rid Effie Mae's house of them cats an' stay there while she's mendin'," Aunt Minnie said. "After all she and he do be kin. He can eat to our house." She emphasized her remarks with a slap on Abe's back.

Abe appeared to relax as rumbles of agreement bounced about.

"Say, I've got to get back to the store," Sidney exclaimed as he jumped up from the kindling box. "Where's my bicycle, Susie?"

So much had happened since I'd dropped it by the cellar door. It took me a minute to recall where I'd left it. "Uh, over by the church cellar steps. I hope it's not dented."

"It'll soon be part of the family, anyway," he replied as he laid his arm on Sarah's shoulder. "And now that I'm acquiring a wife, I've considered buying a tandem.* So, it seems that the bicycle will be available for certain family members, if they're interested, that is," he concluded as he looked at me and smiled.

"Wowee, Sidney! I'll be ever so careful with it. No more cemetery hills—"

"What's a tandem?" little Joe asked, interrupting me.

"Why, that's a bicycle that two can ride," Sidney told him, as he gave Sarah a love-sick smile.

"So, it'll be this kind of marriage," Abby observed. Then, she sang,

Daisy, Daisy,
Give me your answer, do.
I'm half crazy all for the love of you.
It won't be a stylish marriage;
I can't afford a carriage,
But you'll look sweet
Upon the seat of a bicycle built for two.

Everyone but Abe laughed, and Doc pronounced it better than his bicycle song.

The corners of Abe's mouth did seem to lift a little. He might come around to God's way yet if he hung around our house long enough, I thought. Just see how Sidney had changed!

* * *

Life in 1897

ALLERGY TO CATS: The symptoms Abe suffered from his allergy to cat dander affects many people today too. Only back then, it was called asthma and there were no decongestant tablets for treatment.

BETROTHAL: Betrothal is an old-time word for an engagement to be married.

BICYCLES: Bicycles had been around for years, but it wasn't until the late 1880's when the so-called "safety" model was developed. It had pneumatic or balloon tires (tires with air in them). Only then did bicycling become popular nationally. VELOCIPEDE was another name for bicycle. And BONESHAKER was a nickname given to a bicycle because of the many rough roads.

"A BICYCLE BUILT FOR TWO" or "DAISY, DAISY": This song was written in 1892 by Henry

Dacre when bicycles were so much in demand. The *TANDEM* or bicycle built for two was the fashionable way for a young man to transport his girlfriend.

CHURCH: A church was believed to be incomplete unless a bell hung in its belfry (bell tower). In the west, electricity and plumbing were conveniences of the future. So buildings were lit by lamps that burned coal oil or mineral oil kerosene. And "little houses out back" were used in place of bathrooms with plumbing.

COMMUNICATION: With no radios, TV, telephones, or airplanes, news took a bit longer to spread in 1897. This was especially true in out-of-the-way towns like Horseshoe Bend, that didn't even have a railroad track. But the "latest news" arrived eventually, usually in written form or by word of mouth.

COON'S AGE: An expression meaning a long time, since racoons were thought to live a long time.

COURTING: Dating a girl with hopes of marrying her was far more formal in the late 1800s than it is now.

DANDIFIED: Looking or acting like a dandy. A *DANDY* was a man who was overly concerned about looking and dressing nicely.

DECORATION DAY: Memorial Day; the day people decorated graves of loved ones, especially soldiers who have defended the U.S.A.

DEPORTMENT: Another word for behavior or manners.

DOCTOR: Back then almost anybody could tack "Doctor" on the front of his name. He could concoct a pill or brew and bottle it with the guarantee that it would cure everything from spots before the eyes to cold feet. *SNAKE DOCTORS* traveled about selling bottled snake oil, which many believed to be a miraculous cure for all kinds of ailments (sicknesses). Since most of the wonderful drugs we have today were developed after 1900, it's no wonder that people who were suffering fell for the claims made by these "doctors."

DRUGSTORE: A drugstore in the 1890s sold many of the same things a drugstore sells today. The *lady's section* where Sarah worked was necessary because in 1897 a "lady" blushed at the thought of buying "personal items" from a man.

GAIT: Manner of walking or moving—still used, especially when speaking of horses.

GIFT OF GAB: The ability to talk a lot. Gab is another word for chatter or talk.

GOOSE IS COOKED: A way of saying that you're finished or "done for."

HAREBRAINED: Foolish—has a brain the size of a hare or rabbit!

HANKY: Another word for handkerchief. Tissues were unknown in those days. The sign of a well-dressed man was a clean white handkerchief in his coat pocket. Women carried lacy hankies.

HIGHTAIL: To move fast, often to run away. It probably came from the way a deer runs from danger with its tail up in "danger" position.

HORSESHOE BEND: You won't find Horseshoe Bend on an Oregon map. But the town is patterned after any number of small towns in the high desert country of northeastern Oregon.

IRISH: Since Susie's papa (children seldom called their fathers "Daddy" then) and Aunt Minnie are Irish, it shows up in their speech and conduct. Most of the Conroys seem to have inherited their red hair and impulsive, noisy ways from Papa's side of the family.

KINDLING: Small firewood used to start or "kindle" a fire.

LADYLIKE: Growing up to be a well-mannered lady was thought as important as growing up healthy. (Western standards did tend to be a bit slack compared to those in the north and southeast.) A lady obeyed a list of "dos" and "don'ts" such as: 1. A lady never shows or crosses her ankles. 2. A lady never raises her voice. 3. A lady keeps her delicate complexion (skin) protected from the dangerous rays of the sun. 4. A lady is good at embroidery, tatting, knitting, etc. 5. A lady must walk gracefully and *never* run. 6. A lady must *never* call attention to herself by loud talk or laughter. A girl's progress in becoming "a lady" was greatly hampered if she were noisy by nature.

MAGIC LANTERN SLIDES: The polyopticon or magic lantern was the forerunner of our slide projector. Wouldn't you think the machine was "magical" if you'd never seen movies or TV?

MOONING: Spending free time daydreaming.

ODD STICK: A person who doesn't fit in—is unlike others.

ORPHAN: A child without parents who was often raised by a relative.

PARLOR: Formal living room, usually used only for visiting with guests.

PARSON: Pastor, minister, preacher.

PARSONAGE: The house, usually on church property, where the preacher lived. Some churches still have parsonages for their pastor. Another word for parsonage is *manse.*

PENNY THRILLER: A penny thriller was a cheaply written book; low on morals, high on excitement.

ROADS: In the late 1800s, many roads were just dirt, even in towns. Others were gravel. Many city roads were paved with bricks or stones. That meant roads were very bumpy and riding a bicycle could be a real "bone-shaking" experience.

SCIATICA, DYSPEPSIA, INSOMNIA: These are terms used for illnesses. The first refers to a pain in the hip and leg. Dyspepsia is indigestion or stomach upset. Insomnia is the inability to sleep.

SCROOCHED: Huddling down to make yourself as small as possible.

SHENANIGANS: Irish word for pranks or tricks or mischievous behavior.

STOKED UP THE STOVE: Adding fuel—probably wood or coal—to the fire in the stove or building up the fuel so that the fire would last a long time.

STRADDLE AND SKEDADDLE: Straddle meant to sit with a leg on each side of something—in this case a bicycle bar. Skedaddle meant to move, get out, or run away.

TRAVELING SALESMAN: Abe's traveling about, selling from a horse-drawn van, wasn't out of the ordinary at all. Traveling salesmen, who were more frequently called peddlers, packmen, hawkers, bucksters, or drummers, were a common sight during the 1800's. When they called on homes, they were usually welcomed as providers of necessities and news.

UNDERDRAWERS: Underpants.

VAN: Similar to today's vans only they were horse-drawn. An enclosed wagon often made of wood.